Cold As Ice

T. STYLES

NATIONAL BEST SELLING AUTHOR OF RAUNCHY

COLD AS ICE

Are You On Our Email List?

Sign up on our website

www.thecartelpublications.com

Or text the word:

Cartelbooks to 22828

For prizes, contests, etc.

CHECK OUT OTHER TITLES BY THE CARTEL

PUBLICATIONS

COLD AS ICE

WWW.THECARTELPUBLICATIONS.COM

BY T. STYLES   5

COLD AS ICE

By

T. Styles

(Originally Published in 2007)

Library of Congress Control Number:

ISBN 10: 1945240288

ISBN 13: 978-1945240287

Cover Design: BOOK SLUT GIRL

www.bookslutgirl.com

www.thecartelpublications.com
First Edition
Printed in the United States of America

BY T. STYLES   7

CARTEL URBAN CINEMA'S 2nd WEB SERIES

IT'LL COST YOU (Twisted Tales Season One)

NOW AVAILABLE:

YOUTUBE / STREAMING / DVD

www.youtube.com/user/tstyles74

www.cartelurbancinema.com

www.thecartelpublications.com

CARTEL URBAN CINEMA'S 1st WEB SERIES

THE WORST OF US (Season One)

NOW AVAILABLE:

YOUTUBE / STREAMING/ DVD

www.youtube.com/user/tstyles74

www.cartelurbancinema.com

www.thecartelpublications.com

Season 2 Premieres November 15th on

YouTube

BY T. STYLES   9

CARTEL URBAN CINEMA'S 1st MOVIE

PITBULLS IN A SKIRT – THE MOVIE

www.cartelurbancinema.com and

www.amazon.com

www.thecartelpublications.com

COLD AS ICE

#ColdAsIce

BY T. STYLES

11

DEAR READERS,

I wrote this story early in my writing career to be included in a collection for my previous publisher. I believe it sparked the start of my raw story telling nature. I wanted to share it with you under my label.

Enjoy.

T. Styles

PROLOGUE

JUNE 2007

PRESENT DAY

Pepper and Zykia sat on the edge of the bed eyes glued onto Pepper's TV at the horrible sight. And to think, someone she saw everyday was responsible. Someone she didn't necessarily trust, but at least there was no fear, until now.

"Pepper, ya'll ready to eat?" Grace, Pepper's mother yelled from the kitchen.

COLD AS ICE

"Uh...no...ma," she said wiping the tears from her face. "We'll eat later."

"Don't let it get cold," Grace continued. "Ya'll have been in there all day.

But neither of them could eat if they wanted. The scene was extremely violent and had both girls cringing. After more time Pepper stood up and pressed pause on the worst part. She couldn't barely stand tall or look at anymore.

"Calm down, Zy," she responded slowly taking the phone from her hand. "I'm fucked up about this too. But I have a plan."

CHAPTER ONE

DAYS EARLIER

JUST ANOTHER DAY

The sweltering heat didn't stop the beat of the street in Southeast DC. Dudes were washing their cars or moving product, while females were walking up and down the block in the hopes of being seen in their designer fits and purses. While the blood in the veins of 58th avenue's worst project continued to move, 17-year-old Pepper Champagne Thomas was sitting on the steps of her house getting her hair braided, watching it all and hating every bit of it.

COLD AS ICE

A few feet over, two girls who were supposed to be friends were pulling each other's hair out over a boy who didn't want either of them, while their fake friends crowded around.

As she watched, sweat ran down her back causing the white tank top she was wearing to cling to her skin and the black *LRG* sweat pants she was sporting didn't make her much cooler. Ants were circling a piece of melted candy her cousin threw on the ground next to them, and the ice in her cup filled with Coke had dissolved and become tasteless.

It was hotter than a pair of opened legs.

When the fight was over, she wiped sweat off of her face with her hand, Pepper noticed her cousin used an entire pack of red braiding hair in an hour, which was strange considering she was supposed to be doing micro minis, not African twists.

"Nic...I think these too fat! You know I don't lie 'em like that!" Pepper said under her breath trying to avoid confrontation. She was rubbing her fingers over the extra large braids.

She knew the moment Nic's big mouth friend, Treesy called on the phone and broke her concentration, that she'd be too concerned with gossip to tend to her hair.

"Nic, I said these too fat!"

Nic hit her cousin's hand with the yellow rat-tail comb and said, "Hold on Tree."

With that she placed the white cordless phone on her fleshy right shoulder, and held it in place with her fat cheek. Afterwards she gripped a fist full of her baby cousin's unbraided hair.

"First off these ain't too fat!" she said grabbing a few. "And I been braiding hair for ten years so if you don't like 'em, you can take your ass down to the

COLD AS ICE

African Hair Gallery and pay them bitches five hundred dollars, instead of the measly forty your mother giving me!" she pointed with the comb.

"If you don't want to do them right then leave my hair alone."

"You too grown. That's your problem. One day I'm gonna fuck you up out here. Cousin or not."

Without even giving Pepper a chance to respond she resumed the conversation she was having with her ghetto ass friend. Pepper's stomach turned a little when a summer breeze came through, and forced the scent of Nic's corn chip smelling pussy in her face.

Pepper was angry about the bullshit job she was doing on her hair but knew if she bucked, she wouldn't get it done at all, plus she'd have to take out the thirty braids Nic had done so far. She wished she wasn't afraid to speak up.

All her life she let people walk over her and her cousin was no exception.

As Pepper listened to her cousin talk about everybody else except for her own fat ass, she looked around the block. Just then she saw Khoury walking down the street with her best friend's dumb ass brother Jordan and Izzy his other friend, who was nothing but a punk.

"What up, Pepper!" Khoury waved. "What you doing? Getting your self pretty for me?"

Pepper wasn't considered the prettiest girl on the block but she was thick to death. She had a little bit around the waist but her ass made up for it. When you saw her, it was the first thing you noticed. And if there were any doubt it was Pepper, her light skin, bright red hair and freckles would assure you she was coming in the room. People didn't believe her real name was Pepper but it was true. Her mother

COLD AS ICE

had given it to her the moment she saw the freckles throughout her face.

"No!" She rolled her eyes and at him and placed her head down. "Get outta my face, boy."

Zykia, her best friend said she ignored him because she was feeling him. After all, he was easy on the eyes. Khoury was 6'3 with neat dreads and light brown skin. He had them young boy muscles on lock too. Word on the street was that he wrote and sang R&B songs and was new around the way so Pepper didn't understand why he got up with the wrong crew so quickly.

"I told you she dumb as shit," Jordan yelled afterwards throwing a rock her way. "Leave that bitch alone."

"Don't get fucked up, JD!" Nic yelled interrupting her call. "If I get up it's over for you."

"Whatever!" he screamed grabbing at his crotch. "The moment you come over here this fat dick gonna be in that mouth." Jordan and Izzy broke out into heavy laughter.

"That lil boy worthless!" Nic said to Treesy. "How you gonna tell an adult to suck your dick?"

When they were gone, Pepper took a bite of her pickle in a bag. She glanced around and saw empty potato chip bags, beer bottles and drug paraphernalia all around her street. Graffiti decorated all the boarded up houses yet kids played in and around them as if they were playgrounds. Even though she lived in the P.J.'s, every other house had either a Cadillac or a souped up hooptie on 22-inch rims sitting in front of it. Every day she walked out of her door she dreamed of one thing…getting away.

"Pepper, hand me another strand of hair!" Nic yelled breaking her out of her thoughts. Pepper carefully parted a few strands of the red hair from the bundle, so that she could limit the thickness of her braids. Nic snatched it and said, "Give me some more!" Rolling her eyes, Pepper parted a few more strands and handed it to her.

When she took another bite of the sour pickle, she saw her next-door neighbor, and 58th avenue's biggest drug dealer walking to his car.

He was dressed perfectly for the hot weather. Wearing a pair of blue Evisu jean shorts, a white wifebeater and his platinum diamond chain and watch, it was no mistaking that he looked like money. He completed his look with the trademarked original Timbs, most DC natives donned. Ice favored *The Game* greatly.

At 6'2", he had that jailhouse body thing going on strong. Every muscle on his body was formed and he was tattooed from head to toe. But the one Tat that stood out the most was the snake that wrapped around his neck and ended at the tip of his dick. Some people said the snake represented his personality and he never denied it.

On hot days, he'd be outside cleaning up his silver *Aston Martin*, with no shirt on. And all the females young and old would be outside just to catch a glimpse of him.

His mother "Dip" was right by his side sporting a brown *Birkin* bag and a major attitude. They called her Dip because even though she was 36, she had been stripping and *dipping*, up until a year ago. She even looked like *Ronnie*, from *The Players Club* movie but thought she was better looking.

Dip was wearing tight blue *Seven* jeans, a brown tank top, and brown *Prada* sandals. Her waist was still small and her ass was beyond fat. She had a hell of a body to be 5'2 with a bigger mouth to go with it.

As always, Dip sported a blond bone straight weave that hung down her back. Even though nothing was natural about its color, her hair was always fresh. Plenty of niggas would kill for a chance to fuck Ice's mother because she was beyond sexy. But since they valued their lives too, these same niggas left her alone.

Dips high heels could be heard clicking as they walked toward the car. They stepped over *Deadman,* the neighborhood drunk who'd shown up out of nowhere about two months ago. "I'm so sick of this nigga."

"Don't worry about it, ma. He'll be slumping on somebody else's curb soon."

BY T. STYLES 25

She shook her head and Dip waved with her extra long red nails when she saw Nic and Pepper sitting on the steps. "Hey, girls! So what kind of braids you getting today? The fat ones?"

Pepper sighed, because Dip had confirmed that her braids were too big. "Nah, they 'spose to be small." She looked up at her cousin with a side eye.

"Awww...they still cute though," Dip winked.

When Ice saw whom Dip was talking too he opened the car door for his mother and yelled, "What up, Nic? You good?" The passenger door remained open as his mother slid inside. The thick black hair under his arms was shown as he waved.

"Hey,baby." she screamed over Pepper's head. She pressed her mouth against the phone and whispered, "Hold on, Tree. Ice's fine ass out here."

Nic was just like the other girls in the neighborhood when it came to Ice, always on his

COLD AS ICE

dick. As much as Pepper hated his guts she could see why. He was the kind of sexy that only a secure woman could date because every chick he passed dropped their jaws when he walked by.

Ice slammed the door shut. He gripped the top of his pants to pull them up and strolled in Nic's direction. The strings on his Timbs were untied and dragged against the ground and the snake on his neck moved when he did.

He winked when he saw Pepper staring at him and embarrassed, she turned away.

Nic jumped up from behind Pepper, knocking her over with her cheeks just to hug him in the process. The entire back of her grey sweat pants was filled with sweat.

Since Nic was gonna do all she could to talk Ice's head off, Pepper felt she had enough time to get something to drink. Plus her hand had landed in the candy with ants beside her.

She walked into the house, washed her hands, got something to drink and walked back out. Ice was still there. *Shit why didn't he leave? I can't stand him.*

When she saw a baggy dandling in his hands with creamy colored rocks inside she realized what was up. Nic was getting served. They took a few steps forward to each other and Ice placed a 20 sack in her hand. Nic stuffed it in her bra, afterwards turning around to see if Pepper was watching.

She was.

Nic had just taken drugs from Ice.

Caught snooping, she stepped outside. Once there Ice smacked her upside her forehead causing an immediate red bruise. "What's up wit your punk ass?" he joked. "You nosey as fuck!"

"Why you do that?" she said rubbing her head making the mark worse. "That hurt and I'm not bothering you!"

Pepper didn't understand why he insisted on treating her like a kid. If he wasn't slapping her upside her head, he was clowning her in front of everybody on the block.

"Girl, shut up and stop tripping," Nic interrupted as she nudged her cousin in the arm. "He was just playing wit' you. Toughen up."

"Yeah...calm down, girl," Ice laughed. "That mark gonna go away. It ain't like you weren't ugly to begin with."

Ice and Nic both laughed.

"She a mess ain't she?" Nic continued.

When they saw how mad Pepper was, they continued to laugh at her expense until Dip began blowing the hell out of Ice's car horn. "Come on, Ice! I ain't got all day."

He turned to look at her. "One second, ma." He turned back to Nic. "Aight, girl," Ice said after giving her a pound. "I'ma get up with you later." He pointed.

Pepper sat down, eager to get her hair braided and to get rid of her cousin.

"Good looking out, boo," she smiled, taking her seat behind Pepper. When she saw him pull off, she directed her attention to Pepper. "You need to stop acting all funny and shit with Ice," she yelled grabbing her hair. "He ain't gotta speak to you."

"Stop pulling my hair!" Pepper screamed snatching away from her.

"I'm serious! It ain't like he ain't your neighbor," she continued pointing the comb in her face. "Plus he be just playing with your ass because he think you cool. Respect the politicians of the hood."

"So you taking drugs now?" Pepper asked out of nowhere. She couldn't believe she called Nic on her shit, knowing Nic would fuck her up.

"You ain't see shit," Nic said staring at her. "If my mamma tell me you told aunt Grace I'ma beat your ass every day for a week."

Pepper looked at her cousin's face. It was weird how much she looked like her mother. All of the women in Pepper's family had light skin with *some* freckles. But none of them had as many as Pepper.

"Keep your mouth closed, Pepper. I'm serious. And ease up on Ice. He just a man."

"Well I don't like him playing with me like that." Pepper advised as she spotted her best friend walking in her house a few doors down, with her mother who was strung out on crack. "I just want him to leave me alone."

"Keep acting like that and see where it gets you, Pepper." She grabbed her hair and told her to turn around. "All them A's and B's ain't gonna change the fact that you still live in the P.J.s. So *pllleeeeassse* believe, you ain't no better than the rest of us. You gonna always be here, so get use to it." After she finished chastising her, *for what Pepper didn't know*, Nic got back on the phone and ran her mouth until the battery ran dead.

Pepper was relived because she wanted a chance to think. So what she wanted something different with her life. And so what she wasn't sweating Ice like the other girls on the block. Her dreams extended out the hood. Still she thought about what her cousin said repeatedly.

COLD AS ICE

All them A's and B's ain't gonna change the fact that you still live in the P.J.s. So pllleeeeassse believe, you ain't no better than the rest of us. You gonna always be here, so get use to it.

"I might not be better than everybody but I am getting out of here." She said to herself. "I don't care what I gotta do."

CHAPTER TWO

AND THE BEAT GOES ON

"They want more DVD's, Ice," the caller said as they drove down the street. "You got any more?"

Ice sighed. "Naw...but what I tell you bout calling me on this line? You making shit hot."

"Sorry...I called you on the other line but you ain't answer. Figured I'd take my chance and call you here."

"Next time wait till I hit you back!" He said firmly looking at his mother who sat over from him shaking her head.

COLD AS ICE

"You gotta get these niggas in check, son," she whispered. "I keep telling you."

He shook his head and directed his attention back on the call. "Look, tell them perverted mothafuckas they gonna get they movies. Just make sure they wire my money too." He ended the call and placed his Palm Treo cell phone back in the belt clip on his waist.

"You finished?" Dip asked sarcastically.

"Don't start with me, ma. Please."

"Can you trust her?" Dip removed her blush from MAC. When she was done she said, "Cause I don't like a whole lot of people in my business." She turned up the radio the moment she heard Ciara's *"Promise"* playing.

"What do you want me to say?" He shrugged. "She got the connections we need." He sipped on the

Captain Morgan's rum and Coke in his Redskins cup. "And so far she hasn't proven me wrong."

"I sure hope you right, Ice," Dip said pointing her extra long red nail in his face. Dip never cut her fucking nails and because of it, they grew real long and began to curl under. "You trust too many people and one day that's gonna bite you in the ass. Not everybody need direct access to you. It's okay to create space. It makes you more desirable."

"Like I said I got this," he said putting his hand on his chest. "Let me worry about this part of the business. You just make sure the hoppers are supplied with everything they need on the streets." He placed his right hand on the steering wheel and leaned toward his window. "The movies only one side of the picture."

"Yeah whatever," Dip said waving him off now popping a piece of gum. "Just be careful."

COLD AS ICE

Ice hated when Dip ragged on him about handling business. It was because of him she didn't have to strip anymore and as far as he was concerned, she should be grateful.

But, to hear Dip tell it, it was her skills that made him who he was today and anything he earned was as much hers as it was his.

"One of these days when I'm gone you gonna wish you had someone who looks after your back more than me. One day if you not careful you gonna get caught. You better hope I'm there to bail you out."

CHAPTER THREE

THE PRICE OF CURIOSITY

Grace Thomas was throwing down in the kitchen. The two-bedroom row house smelled like fried chicken, rice, string beans and blueberry cornbread. Although Grace worked three jobs, one as a waitress, the other as a maid and her latest job as a security guard in a downtown DC Federal office building, she still managed to cook every night for Pepper.

When dinner was ready, Pepper rushed to the table with a *Home Buyers* magazine in hand. She

COLD AS ICE

wanted desperately to move and continued to search for options.

Her fresh new braids sat in a pony-tail on top of her head. Her scalp was still sore but she didn't mind because the more pain she was in meant the longer they'd last. Sitting at the table she turned around when she heard the anchorwoman on the news say:

And the search for a masked serial rapist continues. He has kidnapped and raped over six young women in the Southeast DC area. The perpetrator is apparently meeting these young women on the popular website Myspace.com. And when they set up a location, he jumps out of his vehicle wearing a mask over his face. Afterwards, all of the victims have been drugged rendering them unconscious.

Although no accurate description of the subject can be given, witnesses do say he is over six feet tall, of African-American descent and has a muscular physique.

Crystal Hyatt, who has been missing for two months, is believed to be one of his latest victims. She was last seen walking toward Addison Road subway station, in Capitol Heights Maryland. If you have any information about this case, please contact authorities immediately.

Hearing about murders and crime wasn't new to Pepper. What was new was the idea of a serial rapist roaming so close to her home. "Mama, that's close. I may know that girl."

"Don't worry about all that." She pointed a long finger in her face. "You and Zykia just be careful out there. I'm thinking about making you stay in the house."

Grace entered the living room wearing her black security guard uniform, no weapon. Out of all the jobs Grace had, Pepper hated the security one the most because she was charged with defending others, without a gun. "Mama, please don't."

"Shut up, Pepper because I ain't made up my mind yet." She paused. "I don't know if they're gonna ever catch that bastard."

"I don't understand." Pepper rose from the table and brought over two large white plates from the kitchen. "Why can't they catch him?"

"I don't know but if they don't, someone else will, rape is horrible." She shook her head. "If I knew who it was I'd cut his dick off myself."

"That's why I'll be glad when we move from around here," she said as Snoop and R.Kelly's "That's, That," video played in the background. Placing the plates down, she grabbed the magazine and flipped to the folded page. "Why can't we move in a house like this one?" She pointed.

Grace glanced down and saw the three hundred thousand dollar home she was pointing to. "Because we don't have *house like this* money."

Pepper closed the magazine and flopped down in the kitchen chair. "It's not fair! People like Ice get to buy whatever they want and we have to struggle just to have a nice place to live!"

"Pepper, we only need two thousand more dollars to put a deposit down on one of those new homes in Alexandria Virginia. With all the overtime I'm doing I'll have that by next month. We are nothing like Ice so it's different."

Pepper frowned and crossed her arms over her chest. "Yeah but the houses may be sold by then."

"Pepper," Grace said exhaling. "You're too anxious. Don't *ever* let people or situations change

COLD AS ICE

who you are just because you desire a thing that God hasn't given you yet. Everything will happen in time. In HIS time."

"Okay, ma." Pepper said ignoring everything she said by rolling her eyes. "If you say so."

"So what's going on with you and that young man?"

Pepper exhaled. "Jai?"

"Yes."

"He's okay I guess." She shrugged, despite him being the reason she had plans later on that night.

"Are you two still fighting?"

"Ma! Why you gotta know what I'm doing with him?" Pepper was embarrassed by her pushiness. "We 'aight."

"Okay," Grace laughed grabbing her car keys. "Whatever you do, don't stay up late. I may come home early so don't be out late."

"Aight, ma."

"I'm for real! I want you in bed by ten, Pepper." She pointed in her face. "Not a minute later."

The minute Grace hit the door, Pepper ran to the phone.

CAUGHT UP

Pepper flopped on the bed and looked at the ceiling, the phone pressed against her ear. "Is Zykia there?"

COLD AS ICE

"Who's this?" Her brother screamed into the phone. Ludacris' "*I Grew Up*", song blasted in the background so Pepper knew their mother wasn't home. "I can't hear you."

She rolled her eyes. "It's Pepper, boy. Is Zykia there or not? Why you acting all crazy?"

"Girl, do you know what time it is?" He yelled. "It's eleven fucking o'clock at night. You don't supposed to be calling this late."

She sighed. "I'm sorry, Jordan. I just wanted to holla at her right quick. Before she went to bed that's all."

"Next time look at a clock before you call here, bitch!"

Pepper heard the phone drop and thought he hung up until she heard her best friend's voice. "Hey, Pepper."

"What's wrong with your brother?" Whenever she saw or spoke to him, he always had something smart to say out his mouth.

"You know how JD is. He mad at the world. But what's up?"

"I want you to go with me to Jai's house tonight," she slid off the bed and looked at a few jeans in her closet. When she couldn't find the pair she wanted, she remembered she wore them yesterday and that they were in the hamper.

"What you suspect this time?"

Pepper ran to the bathroom, opened the lid and smelled the jeans. She lifted them out, concluding they were good. "I think he messing with Diamond or something."

Zykia took a deep breath and said, "Stop tripping, Pepper. You know he hangs with her brother. Of course she's gonna be around."

COLD AS ICE

"Tell Pepper I said hi," Khoury said in the background, interrupting the call.

Pepper smiled when she heard Khoury's voice.

"Khoury told me to tell you hi," Zykia teased.

"I heard him, girl!" Pepper yelled. "Who cares what he says anyway?"

"You over there worrying about Jai when Khoury trying to get with you. He fine, girl! If he wasn't my brother's friend I would try my hand."

"Then go 'head."

"What's wrong with him?"

"He just trying to hit," Pepper said. "Anyway, back to Jai, if everything is cool why when I call over the house she keep hanging up? Everybody at school think they together now so I have to find out for myself. Please."

"Pepper…"

"Come on! You got to roll with me over there."

"I can't. Jordan will have a fit!"

She placed the jeans on her bed and put a white *DC's Finest* baby T a few inches over them, to see how they'd look if she rocked them together.

"I'm your best friend, Zy, please." she whined. "Yesterday Diamond told Caramel at school she wanted him."

"Then why didn't you say that? You made it sound like you weren't sure. Okay...I'll go with you" Zykia gave in. "I'ma meet you in front old lady Howard's house in fifteen minutes. I have to think of a way to shake JD's ass."

"Ewwwww, why her house?"

"Because everything can hide easily over there."

Old lady Howard had the most fucked up house on the block. The fence was broke. The trees in her yard were extra long and extended out of the fence and onto the sidewalk. People couldn't even walk past her house without knocking into branches. It was a perfect place to be incognito as long as her barking dog wasn't outside. Many a drug transaction went down right in front of her property without her knowing.

"You right and I'll see you in a few!"

"Don't thank me yet, Pepper. You know since ma's sick, JD think he's my father so he's going to trip."

Zykia could never admit that her mother was on drugs. She always said she was sick instead but the neighborhood knew the truth.

Pepper couldn't stand Jordan's ass. He'd done everything from robbery to assaulting elderly people for money. But the thing that really caused her to hate him was the night she stayed over their house.

Pepper woke up at one o'clock in the morning because Jordan was pressing his body on top of hers tugging at her panties. He was pulling them so hard to the side that she cried out in pain before he even entered her virgin vagina.

"Shut up you, little bitch," Was all he kept saying.

When she kept fighting he told her over and over to be quiet but she didn't listen. The only reason he stopped trying to rape her was because his mother was home and he didn't want to get caught.

When he heard noise outside the room she was sleeping in that night he said, "If you tell anybody I'll kill you. And then I'll kill your mother." As violent as he was, she knew he meant it.

Excited that Zykia was going with her she said, "Okay...but please do all you can to get out the house."

"I said I will, girl! And bring me a Coke too."

"Got it!" Pepper said excitingly. She didn't know what she was going to do once she saw Jai because for real, she was scary hearted when it came to expressing herself. She was going to think of part two of her plan as they walked the four blocks to Diamond's house.

Pepper put on her outfit with her favorite red Old Navy thong sandals. Afterwards, she grabbed two Cokes, one for herself and the other for Zykia. It took her fifteen minutes to get dressed so she was sure Zykia was already waiting in front of old Lady Howard's broken fence.

The moment she twisted the doorknob, she heard a lot of commotion outside of her house. When she opened the door slightly and peeped out, she saw four men leaving Ice's house in a hurry. One of them looked toward Pepper's house and she slammed the door shut, cutting the lights off too.

Something was off that was for sure and she didn't want to be a witness to what she knew was going down.

A robbery.

When she thought it was safe, she kneeled on the couch under the window and moved the yellow curtains slightly to the side. She saw two men quickly carrying a safe to a van.

Yeah, it was definitely a robbery.

THE HEIST

COLD AS ICE

"Hurry the fuck up!" one of them yelled as they placed the safe in a black van and slammed the door shut. "That bamma may be on his way home and we don't wanna be here when he gets back."

"Nigga, shut the fuck up and bring the rest of that shit in here." The second man replied from the van. "Running your mouth not helping us go quicker. Lift and move. Lift an move."

"Look, slim, you got everything right?" a third man questioned placing two pillowcases full of drugs in the van.

"Everything we need," the fourth replied as a DVD dropped out of the pile of things he had in his hand from Ice's house.

"Let's roll." The second man yelled.

They were in the van when the second man said, "I think somebody was looking out the window in that house." He pointed at Peppers crib. "I'm almost sure of it."

"So what?" The first man said shrugging his shoulders. "Why should we give a fuck? We out." They sped off.

Now an eyewitness, Pepper didn't move until five minutes later. She couldn't believe someone had the nerve to rob Ice's house when they knew how violent he could be.

After waiting sometime, she looked out of the curtain one last time to be sure they were gone and to be sure no one was watching *her* watching them. The streets were clear but when she glanced over at his house, she saw the screen door swinging back and forth making a screeching noise.

Looking around his yard she saw something lying in his grass.

What is that? She thought.

COLD AS ICE

Curious, Pepper jumped up and slowly opened her door. She was still afraid to leave her step so she squinted and saw what appeared to be a white DVD case. Something told her to mind her own business but curiosity got the best of her, so she let it take over.

Pepper slowly stepped down her stairs and ran to his yard. *Go back in the house Pepper.* She tried to tell herself as she ran barefooted from her grass to his. But it was too late. The case was in her hands and there was no turning back.

She dipped back inside, slammed the door and locked it behind herself. Out of breath, her back fell up against the door as she slid to the floor to examine the case.

The phone was in reach from where she sat so she picked it up to call Zykia. "Hey, you won't believe what just happened."

"Where you at?" Zykia yelled. "I was waiting at old lady Howard's fence and her dog started barking and stuff. JD heard that shit and came outside looking for me so I had to go back in. I thought you wanted to see about Jai."

"I do and I'm sorry, Zy but something came up."

"Like what?"

"I just saw Ice's house get robbed and I picked up what I found."

"You lying!"

"I'm not." She looked down at the DVD case in her hand. "It looks plain though."

"Well what is it? You not saying enough!"

"It looks like a DVD or CD case."

"You had me thinking it was something else. It's probably just music," Zykia laughed. "You know every nigga in the hood got a mix tape."

"You're probably right."

"And you better be careful, Pepper. Ice will kill you if he finds out you got something that belongs to him. CD or not."

"I know." She took a deep breath. "I'll call you later."

Before Zy could finish talking Pepper hung up and placed the phone down. She'd opened the case and examined it.

It was a DVD.

If it's a home movie or something I'll just give it back to Ice. Maybe he'll give me a reward. She thought.

She stood up and walked toward her DVD player and put it inside. Just when she hit play, her phone rang. "Hello," she said uninterested at whomever was calling. Her eyes remained on the TV, which was loading.

"You busy?"

It was Jai.

"Actually I am," she responded no longer caring about where he was or who he was with. The DVD was loading. "Can I...uh...call you back?"

"Diamond said you called over here fifteen times, Pepper. And when I hit you back all of a sudden you don't wanna talk?" He asked breaking her concentration.

"If you were so concerned why didn't you get the phone then?" She blurted out. She was surprised in herself.

"What you just say to me?"

"You know what, Jai, now is really not a good time. I mean, can I call you back?"

"Don't call me, I'll call your ass." He said with an attitude before hanging up.

Pepper didn't care.

The phone dropped out of her hands and onto the floor. The DVD had loaded and she couldn't believe her eyes. She was watching the most brutal thing she ever saw in her life. So brutal that tears fell from her sockets. If only she would've left the DVD where it was, she would not have known this dark secret.

There was no turning back now.

CHAPTER FOUR

THE BLAME GAME

Kris was sitting on the floor with his dick in a dog's bowl. His penis was covered with fresh ground beef...Crunch's favorite. Crunch was an orange colored pitbull that was salivating badly because he had not eaten.

They were in Ice's basement.

Sweat poured down Kris's forehead and he couldn't move because his hands were tied behind his back and he was duct taped to the wall.

"So let me get this straight," Ice said standing over Kris, as Dip held Crunch's black leather leash firmly. The dog was barking loudly and moving crazily trying to get at his meal. When the dog got too ridiculous, Dip kicked him and he yelped loudly and lied down. "It just so happened the moment these niggas run up in my crib you at the fucking carry out and don't know or see anything?"

"I swear its true, Ice! I would never play you like that." Kris cried. He was covered in sweat. "We go way back, man. Don't do this to me." He continued looking at the dog that was waiting for Ice's patience to run thin. "I know how you are and I ain't never been crazy enough to mess with you or your property."

"Fuck this nigga, baby," Dip yelled begging him to allow her to release Crunch. She looked at her son and talked calmly. "He just trying to play you like the rest of these clowns. Don't be no fool. If you let him go you might as well give a pardon to the rest of these mothafuckas out here because they gonna try you next." She paused. "I'm telling you straight up, this nigga was in on it." She pointed at Kris with her curly nail.

Ice was furious.

As he stared at Kris sitting naked on his living room floor shivering, he wondered how much of what his mother was saying was true. He wasn't worried about the money or the drugs they got in to him for. He never kept more in that house than he could afford to lose. Ice was more concerned about the DVD that was missing. He kept it under the safe, beneath a floorboard and now it was gone.

"Hold up, Dip," Ice said looking at his mother who was pleading with him to let his dog rip into the man's body parts. "Let me hear this fool out."

"You go be a fool than." Dip shook her head in disgust. She got off on violence.

"I'ma ask you again...do you know who ran up in my place?" He questioned as he stooped down to face him. "Cuz if you don't know something, I'ma let Crunch loose and you'll be *dickless*. You best be telling me what I need to hear, man," he continued.

"Ice, look at me. Don't you think if I knew something I would say it. I didn't have no parts of this man."

The messed up part was that he was telling the truth.

"You know what..." Without even waiting for Ice's approval, Dip released the pit bull onto him. Crunch tore into the meat and his penis.

The pain grabbed Chris at first and then shock of seeing the dog rip at him caused him to pass out.

Livid at his mother's disobedient nature, Ice turned toward her around angrily. He didn't give the okay because he had more questions but now it was too late..

"Why the fuck would you push off until I gave the okay?"

"You already know."

"Just couldn't wait, huh?" Ice asked.

"Why would I?" she smiled. "Waiting's for fools."

A SECOND OPINION

THE NEXT DAY

COLD AS ICE

Pepper was walking by Ice's house on the way to hers when she heard screams coming from inside. She stopped in her tracks after hearing the cries followed by bullets ringing out. Figuring whatever was going on had something to do with the night before she quickened her pace leaving Jai, who was walking with her a few steps behind.

"What in the fuck was that?" Jai asked upon hearing the screams and bullets. "I ain't know the neighborhood kicked off like that."

"I don't know what it is, Jai and we should be minding our business," Pepper responded even further ahead of him to her house. "All I want to do is get inside."

When Pepper passed Ice's car she took a quick glance. It wasn't fair that people like him got to live the good *life* while she and her mother struggled.

Pepper was aware of the four-car garage house he owned in Virginia and his other three cars. The house in DC was nothing more than a business location, to stay close to his dough and niggas on his payroll. She hated him for shitting where she lived.

"Besides, it's probably nothing, Jai," she said.

"Then why the fuck you rushing again?" Jai continued noticing she had been on edge ever since they left school earlier.

Jai didn't believe in rushing and everything with him had to be cool, smooth and slow. They called him Lil Jay Z at school and his relaxed attitude was one of the reasons Pepper fell for him. Although he was two inches shorter than she was, standing 5'5 inches tall, he had a huge personality. His honey brown skin, low hair cut with connecting goatee made him look older than 16. Wearing black sweats, a white t-shirt, with red, yellow and black Bapes

COLD AS ICE

tennis shoes, he walked as if he didn't have a care in the world.

"I thought you were thirsty," Pepper smiled trying to be cool. "Can we just hurry a little? I don't want my mother coming home with me out here." She continued knowing that if her mother came home, her being outside would be the least of her worries.

It would be Jai she would have to explain about.

Now in front of her house, Jai took his time walking up Pepper's stairs. She opened the door and he followed...slowly.

She threw her red book bag on the couch and locked the door. Next, she did a quick run through to be sure her mother wasn't home. Normally she never was, but with what she wanted to show him she had to be extra sure.

While Pepper busied herself with a few details, he sat on the couch grabbed the remote and turned on the TV.

"Before I forget, I heard that nigga got robbed," he said as he scanned through the channels.

Pepper stopped in her tracks, her eyes two sizes larger.

"W…wha..what are you talking about?"

"Stop playing," Jai laughed as he turned on MTV Jams and dropped the remote. "You live right next to this nigga so I know you know something. They saying some dude got him for the dope and his money."

"Oh…oh yeah," she giggled. "You talking about Ice. Uh…yeah…I heard something happened over there." She continued picking her book bag up off the couch.

"So did you see anything?" He asked irritated at how weird she was acting. "Because you look like you went through his crib."

She sat down beside him, trying to think of a good lie.

"Naw...I was sleep." She scratched at the rows between her braids. "I ain't hear nothing."

He frowned. "Hold up...how you gonna be sleep when you was calling me all night?" He continued.

"I can't remember what I was doing last night, Jai," she said clearing her throat. "But I want to show you something." she paused. "I'm kinda scared though."

He sat up straight. "Pepper, I told you I'd be easy on you," he said turning off the TV. Now that he thought she was *finally* going to let him hit, he was suddenly interested in what she had to say. "You can trust me, you know that right?"

"I'm not talking about sex, Jai," Pepper exhaled as she unzipped her book bag removing the DVD. She looked at him again trying to determine if she should show him or not. "I found something the night Ice's place got robbed. This is what I want you to see.""

"So you *were* up?"

"Yes," she continued as she stood up to place the DVD in the player. "Since you wanna be technical and shit."

Jai, knocked it out her hand and said, "Man I'm not trying to see no fucking DVD! You know what I want and I'm tired of you playing games with me, Pepper." He yelled. "Are we fucking or not? You been holding out on me for six months like I'm some sucka ass nigga."

She picked the DVD up off the floor and placed it on the glass living room table, keeping her eyes on

70 **COLD AS ICE**

him the entire time. He'd blown up at her before but never like this.

"So now you mad at me?"

"What you think?"

She took a deep breath. "Please don't be mad. I really have to show you something." Her voice was barely above a whisper.

"You know what," he said getting up. "My boys told me not to fuck with your ass and I should have listened. You ain't nothing but a mothafucking tease! When you asked me over I finally thought I was gonna get some and it was all a game. I'm out of here," he continued as he walked toward the door.

"Don't leave, Jai," she cried grabbing his hand. "I don't have anybody else to talk to about this."

"Get the fuck off me." He pushed her to the floor. She bumped her head on the glass table causing it to bleed a little. "Don't call me no more either." He pointed at her. "I'm fucking Diamond now anyway."

Jai walked out and Pepper cried on the floor.

NO MORE WISER

Ice had a few dudes pick up Kris' bodily remains that were packed inside of three Glad bags. He and Dip watched from the couch as they cleaned up the mess. At some point Chris regained consciousness after the dog ate his penis and Ice put him out of his misery by shooting three bullets in his head.

"I think I fucked up." Ice took a deep breath and looked over at his mother. "I should've been more careful."

"Yes you did, but now we have to find that DVD," Dip whispered.

When the *pick up* boys left she and Ice fired up a blunt. Dip glanced over to the kitchen to look at Pipes and Dro, Ice's friends. "And quick," he said.

"It's dangerous..."

"But ain't nobody watching no DVD, ma," Ice responded as he sipped on the beer and looked toward the kitchen too. Dro who had been slinging for Ice for ten years was playing dominoes with Pipes, his cousin.

"Why you say that?" Dip said fluffing her hair with her nails.

"Think about it, they came for the money not a DVD. Don't nobody but me, you and them mothafuckas in Cali know what we got going on with them DVDs."

"How you know?" She whispered pointing her blunt at him. "Think about it? Why would they take it out the floorboard if they didn't want it?" She blew smoke in the air and passed the weed to him. "You have to be smarter Ice. Like I raised you."

"I am smarter."

"You sure about that?" She asked with raised eyebrows.

"Yes." He confirmed accepting the hand off. "That's why I think we good. If they do find it, they gonna think it's a porno or some shit like that. Chill out."

"Listen, Ice," she yelled forgetting they had company. This time Dro and Pipes looked in their

COLD AS ICE

direction. "You got a problem?" She asked them. They shook their heads. "Well turn the fuck around then." When their attention was totally off of her she continued. "Like I said…you have to be smart about this shit. That little bitch they looking for is on that DVD. That means if it gets in the wrong hands, we're through. And I'm not going to jail for no murder shit, Ice. Not even for my own son."

Ice tried to hand her back the blunt but she waved him off. Instead she grabbed her purse searching for something else. When she found a rolled up napkin with tiny red pills inside she got exactly what she wanted…the "E".

Realizing she didn't have anything to swallow the pill with, she snatched Ice's beer can and tried to swallow the pills. It wasn't enough. "Dro, bring me a Coke from the fridge."

Dro stood up and looked at her for a moment, wanting to tell her to get the fuck out of his face, but thought better of it. "Aight," he said opening the fridge and walking the drink to her. Dro, who was white mixed with black was extremely tall and loyal to Ice but hated Dip's ass with a passion. After handing her the Coke, he stomped back to the table.

"Since we talking about suspects, how you know Dro's ass ain't have nothing to do with it?" she whispered pointing her red manicured nail at Dro as he returned to the kitchen table with Pipes.

Ice frowned. "Cuz them my niggas that's how I know," he responded putting her back in her place. "Look don't reach too far, ma. Them my peoples so trust me, they ain't involved."

"I don't know if you had a chance to look but them ain't no niggas. They half breeds and they'll roll on you in a heartbeat." She snapped her fingers. "I don't trust them."

"They ain't have shit to do with it," he said firmly. "You always coming down on me like I don't know how much shit can kick off if that DVD shows up in the wrong hands. Right now it's out there and until it surfaces we have to deal with not knowing."

"Ice, you better have this shit under control." She pointed at him. "Cause I'm going off on you if it crashes down around us."

"I do...I do."

CHAPTER FIVE

ANOTHER KIND OF CRIMINAL

Pepper and Zykia sat on the edge of the bed eyes glued onto Pepper's TV. Zykia had her hair in two pigtails wearing pink pajamas and was a cute short but thin girl who looked as if she was mixed with Indian and black. Pepper was right beside her wearing a long t-shirt with sweat pants.

It was supposed to be a sleepover but it was anything but. They couldn't believe what they were seeing. Pepper watched it ten times and felt like the first time, *every* time.

COLD AS ICE

"Pepper, ya'll ready to eat?" Grace yelled from the kitchen waking them out of the stupor they were in. The sound was completely down on the TV.

"Uh...no...ma," she said wiping the tears from her face. "We'll eat later."

"Well don't let it get cold," Grace continued. "Ya'll have been in there all day and its time to come up and get some air."

"Okay, mama we will," Pepper replied as she got up to lock the door, just in case her mother got the urge to bust in on them. Afterwards Pepper turned the sound back up a little.

When she returned to the bed, she saw the part where Ice was on top of a young girl. Her naked body was tied to the bed as he repeatedly raped her over and over again, pushing her legs so far apart it looked as if they would break. In the background they heard a woman's voice coaching and encouraging. And since Dip was always with Ice, Pepper recognized it to be her. When a portion of her long nail appeared in front of the camera, it was confirmed.

"Just smile, sweetheart and enjoy yourself," Dip said to the young girl. "This DVD is going to be seen around the world." She laughed. "You'll be a star, we'll see to that."

"Damn this young bitch's pussy tight as shit." Ice responded as the girl cried out, begging him to stop. "She may be the best one, ma. That's for sure."

Dip giggled. "Well enjoy yourself. You killing it."

"I can't believe this is happening," Zykia said. "This...this can't be real."

COLD AS ICE

"It is," Pepper said.

The scene was extremely violent and had both girls cringing as Ice pounded into her like a maniac. The girl was clearly around their age and this made the scene all the more real to them. The sheets were covered in blood but he didn't care.

Instead of letting her go Ice placed his entire mouth over hers and kissed her harshly. His jeans were down at his ankles and his body was sweaty. What gave his identity away was not his face, because it couldn't be seen. It was the snake tattoo that ran from his neck, across his back and ending on this penis. He looked like a monster.

"Pepper...this is serious," Zykia said wiping the tears from her face again. "We have to tell somebody." She looked at the TV once more. "He's...he's hurting her and she's crying."

Pepper moved closer, her eyes widening. "Who we gonna tell, Zy?"

"Uh...how about the police?" She replied sarcastically as she cleared her throat. "Look at what he's doing? I mean, I can't believe you waited this long. We have to say something now. Maybe we can save her, she could still be in his house." She continued reaching for the phone.

Pepper stood up and pressed pause which stopped on the part in which Ice was licking between the frightened girl's legs.

"Calm down, Zy," she responded slowly taking the phone from her hand. "I'm fucked up about this too. But I have a plan."

COLD AS ICE

"You have a plan?" Zykia repeated. "What are you talking about? You're not making any sense."

"Do you know why my mother is still here? Instead of at work?" Pepper asked, as her face turned red. "She's still here because she lost her third job today. That means we can't get the new house. That means I can't leave this fucking place, Zy and I'm tired of being around here."

"Pepper what you talking about?" Zykia asked as she stood up. "You living around here ain't got nothing to do with that DVD. At least your mother ain't all strung out and shit like mine." She added. "I would give anything to live in your house instead of my brother's."

"I want more than this place, Zy." Pepper said ignoring her comment. "A lot more. I'm sorry that you have a lot going on at your house but this can't be my life."

Silence.

"What does that mean?" Zy shrugged. "Because you said you have a plan and I don't hear it yet."

Pepper paced in front of the bed. "I say we get paid for this shit," she pointed looking at the TV. "And we get paid big."

"What?" Zy yelled.

"Think about it for a minute, Zy, " Pepper continued as she paced the room. "He knows the DVD is missing *so*...he'll probably be looking for it. He don't want nobody to find it."

"But he won't be able to find it because the police will have it," Zykia advised. "Right? Because that's what's right."

"And then what, Zy? He pays some high priced lawyers and gets off easy." She pointed at the window. "You know how shit works. How many niggas been locked up for doing shit only to get out two days later?" She sat next to her. "But we can make him pay for this." She pointed at her and then herself. "Us."

Silence.

"And guess what will happen when he finds out who snitched, Pepper? He'll kill us. And I don't know about you but I'm not ready to die."

"Pepper, what's going on in there?" Grace yelled as she knocked on the door. "I thought you were coming out to eat."

"Oh shit," she whispered clearing her throat. "Nothing, ma! We...we were just talking."

"Well talk a little lower," Grace responded. "I can hear ya'll all the way out here."

Pepper knew that wasn't true because she'd be in there asking a whole lot of questions instead of yelling at the door. "Aight, ma, we'll keep it down," Pepper responded before turning back to Zykia. "Like I said, we should get paid," she continued whispering. "I'm tired of seeing Ice with diamonds and new clothes while we're walking around here looking a hot mess."

Silence.

COLD AS ICE

"This is scary to me." She said waving her hand in her face. "And I don't want no parts of this."

"It doesn't have to be...so I propose," she continued when she felt Zykia wasn't buying in. "We blackmail him."

"Pepper...you sound crazy! Aren't you scared of what could happen if we fuck with Ice? Aren't you scared of what he could do to you or your mama? Or to me?"

"And don't you want your own money for a change? Ain't you tired of relying on JD for money and then having to hear his mouth?"

Zykia shook her head no.

"Look at your shoes, Zy." She said picking her Nikes off the floor. "They run down. Don't tell me you want to roll like this." She tossed them down. "You get messed with at school more than I do because of how you dress."

Zykia was no longer rebellious. She thought about having to wear the same banged out clothes day after day and having to wash them in the sink by hands. She shared her panties with her mother and who knew where or who she'd been with. Suddenly the idea of getting a little something for nothing started to sound good to her.

"Pepper," Zykia said breathing heavily. "What will stop Ice from killing us? I mean…if he finds out we're blackmailing him he will end our lives. By his own hands too!"

Pepper could hardly be still she was moving around so much. Besides her best friend was coming around. "No he won't because we will be smart."

"How do you know?"

"Because he won't know it's us. Trust me, Zykia, I've thought about this long and hard. We can do this."

CHAPTER SIX

THE ULTIMATE DISRESPECT

"Ya'll get from around my house," Grace said as she came home early to find three knuckleheads drinking on her steps, shooting dice. They had liquor bottles spread out everywhere.

"Why you always fucking with us?" Knucklehead One said. "We ain't bothering you."

"I'm serious! Leave!" She said as she pushed past them with her purse in one hand, a brown paper bag

COLD AS ICE

filled with groceries in the other. "You in my way and you don't live here."

"I said we rolling out," Knucklehead Two added. "Let me get this money first."

"You wish you were gonna get this money," Knucklehead One yelled, clearly intoxicated and not budging.

"You sound crazy," Knucklehead Three responded as they all laughed. "I'm 'bout to break all ya'll. Just give me five seconds." He continued holding up five fingers.

"I'm gonna call the cops!" She continued. "I don't want my daughter seeing all this!"

"You talking 'bout Pepper's fine ass?" Knucklehead Two asked. "She look like she been eating real good lately," he laughed smoking a Black and Mild with one hand stroking his dick with the other. "What you feeding her? Wheaties?" He looked into her brown paper bag.

"What's wrong with you young men?" She asked snatching the bag away from him. "I changed half of ya'll pampers and you've gotten so disrespectful over time."

"You ain't change my pamper," Knucklehead One laughed giving the second one dap.

"Everything okay, Ms. Thomas?" Khoury asked seeing what was going on in front of her house. They looked at him and stood up. He pulled his cap down and took one step forward, clearly ready to back up his question despite being outnumbered. "You need help with anything?"

"Everything 'aight lil nigga," Ice said walking over to the group out of nowhere. He removed Khoury's cap and placed it on sideways.

COLD AS ICE

"I'm talking to Ms. T." Khoury bucked. He looked at Ice, placed his cap on correctly and then waited for Grace's response. "Are you okay, ma'am? Can I help with anything?" His question was firmer than before.

"Yes, son," she smiled. "I'm fine. Go ahead home."

Khoury looked at Ice once more and walked off.

Ice smirked making mental notes to check his lil ass later. "What ya'll doing out here on this lady's steps?" Ice continued stepping up to the men. When they didn't respond he said, "I asked ya'll a mothafucking question! What ya'll doing out here?"

"Nothing man," Knucklehead One said picking up their things. "We leaving now."

"Well make it quick then!" When they didn't move fast enough due to being scared he yelled, "BOUNCE!"

Hearing the anger in his voice they hurried down her steps. When they were gone he directed his attention to Grace. She looked him over and noticed he looked especially *Icey* with his diamond watch and platinum chain. He was also wearing a red button down shirt that exposed his white wife beater.

She nodded once. "Thank you, son."

He waved the air. "Nah, I'm just sorry 'bout that, man. These youngin's today don't know the first thing about respect." He wiped his mouth with his hand. "I'll make sure that don't happen again, with you being my next door neighbor and all." He pointed in the direction the boys went with his thumb.

He went to help her with her grocery bag but she snatched it away and said, "What you want with me, Sherrod?" She was one of the few people alive that

COLD AS ICE

knew his full name was Sherrod Davis. His evil presence made her extremely uncomfortable. "The children are gone I don't need more trouble on my doorstep."

"Damn, Ms. T. I'm not the enemy," he smiled. "I just got rid of them, or have you forgotten already?"

"I've been knowing you since Dip got a hold of you," she responded slowly and carefully. She was trying her best not to let him see her fright. "And you ain't never known me to play games so I'm not gonna start now. I think you turned for the worse and I don't want you around me too closely. Now it's obvious something's on your mind so I would appreciate the truth."

"I can respect that," he continued smiling. "Well I'ma be straight up with you. Did Pepper mention anything to you 'bout last week? I don't care how small it was."

"Pepper?" She responded quickly. "I don't know what you talking about but Pepper's a good girl. She don't get involved in all this mess out here in these streets. All she does is play with her friend."

"You not answering my question."

"No, she ain't say nothing about you. And if she would've seen anything pertaining to you she would've told me."

"I sure hope you right," he continued. "Cuz I like Pepper, but I'd hate to find out you lying to me."

"Are you threatening me?" She asked her entire body trembling.

Ice took two steps closer to her. She could smell his cologne. "Naw, Ms. T. I would *never*, threaten you," he said calmly. "I would fucking kill you and your daughter too." He wiped her hair behind her ear. "Remember that."

Silence.

COLD AS ICE

Horrified, Grace backed up, walked inside her house and slammed the door, locking it behind her. Slowly she moved to the window and he was still watching the house.

She made up her mind that she had to get Pepper out of that neighborhood, if it was the last thing she did.

OUTSIDE OF THE HOUSE

There was a knock at Ice's door and he stepped toward it. "Who is it?"

"Hey, Ice. It's us."

Ice looked out his peephole and opened his door when he saw who was on the other side. "Did we do everything right?" Knucklehead One asked who was at Grace's house harassing her. "We ain't go too hard did we? You looked like you were mad for real."

"You did a good job." He looked at her house and then back at him. "But why you come straight over here? I told you to wait a minute before you came back. She might have seen your dumb ass."

"Sorry, man. The fellas wanna get something to eat from Lenny's and we ain't got no money. They wanted me to ask now."

"Yeah whatever," he responded waving them off. "But ya'll not finished yet."

Knucklehead One frowned. "What you mean? You told us to sit on her steps and fuck with her

COLD AS ICE

when she got home. That's what we did. Even got in her face when she tried to get us off the steps."

"Like I said, that wasn't the whole deal. You 'spose to be cleaning my car too."

Knucklehead One looked at Ice with disgust. When they made the deal he knew he didn't say anything to them about cleaning his ride, but he wasn't bold enough to challenge him on it. He removed his cap, scratched his head and said, "Aight, Ice, what time you want us here tomorrow?" He placed his cap back on.

"Tomorrow? I want you here tonight." He looked him up and down. "And make sure you get the rims too. 'Aight?"

Knucklehead One nodded in agreement.

After Ice was sure he understood, he handed him fifty dollars to split amongst the three of them. It was seventy-five dollars shorter than the agreement.

"The bucket on the side of my house and the cleaning supplies will be in the trunk. And it'll be open." He yawned. "Now hurry up back before I fuck ya'll up out here. I want my shit spotless."

As Ice walked back in the house and slipped into the bed with a young thing he picked up at the bus stop earlier, he thought about Pepper. For some reason she'd been on his mind a lot and he couldn't understand why.

Lying on top of the bed he rubbed his belly and looked at the ceiling.

"Is everything okay?" She asked as she wrapped her thick tender legs over him.

"Yeah...finish doing what you were doing."

"No problem, daddy." She slid under the covers and wrapped her mouth around his penis.

As she went to work, he thought about Grace. He knew Pepper didn't know anything about the robbery but he had to cover all angles. In the past he never had anything against Pepper, as a matter of fact, he had plans to fuck her but Grace played her too close for his taste.

He put those ideas out of his mind. Business was business and whoever got in the way had to be dealt with.

And that went for Pepper and Grace too.

CHAPTER SEVEN

PLAN INTO ACTION

"Zykia, this gotta be right! You can't be acting all scared and shit!" Pepper said to her on the phone as she looked out her window waiting for Ice to appear. Instead all she saw was Deadman lying on the ground in his usual drunk behavior.

"I don't think he gonna go for it," Zykia responded hesitantly. "He too smart for this shit and I'm starting to have second opinions."

"How you know he won't go for it?" Pepper released the curtain to focus on what she was saying.

COLD AS ICE

"If he was real smart he would've put the DVD somewhere safe. Now say your lines again."

Pepper sat on the edge of her bed listening attentively to be sure she got the lines correct. "That was good, when you call do it just like that."

"I will." She paused. "But where you get his number from?"

"Nic's phone when she came over last night to see my mother." Pepper giggled. "She didn't even know it was gone." She paused. "Now you ready?

"Wait...can we go over the lines once more?"

Pepper rolled her eyes.

"Yeah...go 'head."

"Can I speak to Ice?" Zykia asked disguising her voice.

"This him," Pepper responded in a deep voice roll playing. "Who this?"

"Don't worry about that," Zykia replied. She was more confident than the other times they rehearsed and even added a little seduction. "I got something you want, really bad. You might even be willing to pay for it."

"And what's that?" Pepper said.

"A DVD. *Your* DVD. And to get it back it's gonna cost you."

"I'm listening," Pepper continued. "How much?"

"I want you to pack twenty-five large into a McDonald's paper bag. Then I want you to take it to Addison Road subway station and buy a Metro pass. When you get the pass, I want you to go to the section upstairs by the trains and place the bag in the trash can next to the map. After that, I want you to walk your fine ass back outside, get in your car and go home. Got it?"

"PERFECT!" Pepper yelled jumping up. "You don't sound nothing like yourself. He won't know who you are! Just remember to tell him when he makes the drop his DVD will be at home waiting. Make sure he don't try to follow you cause it'll make the news instead."

"Okay, Pepper," Zykia responded breathing heavily. "I hope you're right about this."

"Just trust me," she replied. "But look...he's outside now! Call him in five seconds." She hung up on Zykia and ran for the front door. "I have to throw him off our tracks."

Without waiting for Zykia to respond, Pepper rushed out the door and closed it behind herself. Ice was standing next to his vehicle placing car cleaning supplies in the trunk. She took one deep breath and walked down the steps, remaining on her own property.

"Hey, Ice," Pepper said softly.

Ice turned around and slammed his trunk closed.

"Aw shit," he joked. "Look at lil big head ass Pepper." He went to smack her upside the head but she pushed his hand away. "I see you quick today," he frowned before a smile settled on his face. "What's up?"

"Have you seen my mamma?"

"Have I seen your mamma?" He repeated placing his keys in his pocket. "Who I look like? Your pappi?"

She laughed loudly, doing her best to procrastinate while wondering why Zykia hadn't called his phone yet. She needed her to call while he was in her face to prove to Ice the call hadn't come from her. *I hope you didn't chicken out on me Zy.* She thought. If the plan didn't go through, it never would because she couldn't see holding a conversation with Ice again.

"I'm just asking because she was supposed to be home by now to take me to the store." She looked up the block. "I guess I'm just kind of hungry."

"I'll ride you," he said licking his lips. "Would you like that?"

Immediately thoughts of the girl he raped entered her head. But before she could respond he threw his index finger up in her face, indicating for her to wait a moment. *"It's Okay"* by The Game rang from his phone. Stepping a little to the side, he answered the call. "Who this?"

Silence.

He looked up the block and waited for the caller to respond. "Yo, what you just say to me?" He walked further away from Pepper.

Silence.

BY T. STYLES 107

Pepper's heart began to thump wildly. Suddenly she realized there was no turning back. Maybe she was out of her league after all when it came to her plan. What made her think she could blackmail one of DC's most notorious dealers? Ice murdered at least six people that she was aware of and the thought had her uncomfortable. She started sweating but wiped her face with her hands hoping Ice didn't notice. And as if that wasn't enough, suddenly she felt faint.

Still on the phone, he turned around and faced her. Pepper tried to maintain the innocent look he'd known her for but it was difficult. "I see...," he responded slowly to the caller, still eyeing Pepper. "And if I don't what will happen then"?

Silence.

COLD AS ICE

"Alright, alright. You'll get your money," he replied. "But you better hope I never find out who you are."

With that he hung up, still staring Pepper down. She knew it was over so she started saying the Lord's Prayer in her head. Her only wish was that she was able to tell her mother goodbye. For some reason, she looked down at Deadman as if he could save her, but he could barely save himself.

"Listen, shawty," he said as if he was madder than the devil himself. "I can't take you to no store. I got some shit to handle so get the fuck outta my face."

And just like that...he walked off. *Did I actually get away with it?* She thought as she watched him walk into his house, slamming the door behind himself.

She didn't waste any time when he was out of view. She had to be sure Zykia was okay. She rushed inside her house, picked up the phone and called but she didn't answer the phone. Pepper called five more times and still she could not get through to her due to the phone ringing busy.

"I guess I gotta wait," she said nervously, sitting on the sofa. Suddenly her phone rang and Pepper anxiously snatched it up. "Zykia! What happened?"

"Pepper, ask your mother if I could wash two loads of clothes over there," Nic said.

CLICK!

Pepper didn't have time for her cousin's shit. She called Zykia again and it felt like forever until she finally answered the phone. "Hello."

"Zykia, what happened?" Pepper asked out of breath. "Are you okay?"

"No," Zykia responded suddenly crying. "I feel so bad for what I did. Something's gonna happen to us."

"It's gonna be alright," Pepper consoled. "If he knew it was us he would've said something to me when I was in his face." She stood up from the sofa and paced the floor.

"That's not it Pepper" Zykia advised.

Pepper remained in place. "Then what is it?"

"Somebody knows."

Silence.

"Somebody like who?" Pepper asked, her heart pounding from her chest. "P...Pepper, just come over and bring the DVD. Please."

Click.

Pepper looked at the phone and placed it back against her ear. "Hello...hello?"

There was no use.

Zykia was gone and Pepper was shook.

CHAPTER EIGHT

A WHOLE DIFFERENT

GAME

Nervous, Pepper bent the corner to her best friend's house. The moment she did she saw a boy she didn't fuck with standing on Zykia's porch.

"What's up, Pepper?" Lil John, a neighborhood youngin' questioned.

"Nothing...why?" She asked nervously. After hearing the fright in Zykia's voice on the phone everything had her shook.

"I'm just asking, damn," he said jogging down the steps and shaking his head. "Reds acting crazy today." He walked up the block.

When he was gone, Pepper knocked softly on Zykia's door. She took one last look behind her to be sure Ice wasn't there ready to smoke her. When she saw he wasn't, she knocked harder but instead of Zykia opening the door, JD did.

"Uh...hey...is...is Zy home?" She stuttered, looking over his shoulder and into the house.

"Now why you acting all scared and shit, girl?" He responded nicer than normal. "Me and you cool," he said opening the door fully. "So it's time we start acting like it."

Silence.

Pepper glanced harder inside and now she could see Izzy, one of his friends who stayed trying to play hard. Khoury was also with him. Within seconds

114   **COLD AS ICE**

Zykia appeared from behind JD and she was crying as usual.

"You gonna come in so we can get down to business or what?" JD asked opening the screen door wider.

WALKING INTO THE

FIRE

"You can't go!" Dip yelled walking up behind Ice. "This ain't nothing but a set up!" She paced the living room floor before stopping suddenly. "The cops probably gonna be there waiting on you. Then they gonna get me too."

"Dip, what you talking about?" Ice asked as he sat on the couch with his face in his hands. "What you want me to do, risk this person having the DVD and not knowing who it is?"

"I want you to wait, Ice."

"For what? The bitch said she got the DVD! Ain't shit to wait on."

"Fuck, they probably didn't even know it was you until you admitted to it!"

"Dip," he paused. "If it was the cops they'd be in here already not blackmailing me for money. Now I say we pay these mothafuckas and get it over with."

"Then what?"

"Get the DVD in our hands and find out who had the nerve to fuck with me. Once I know who it is I'm gonna put them out of they misery," he sighed.

COLD AS ICE

"In the meantime what's twenty-five G's? I'm getting off easy."

Dip threw herself on the couch and went through her purse. Ice knew exactly what she was searching for, an "E" pill.

"You need to stop popping them mothafucking pills! They fuck with your head and we need to be thinking straight right now," he continued as he poured himself a glass full of Captain Morgan's straight up.

"And you don't need to be telling me what to do when you drink that shit like its water. I should've never got caught up in this porno DVD bullshit." She yelled spit escaping her mouth. "We were getting money already moving the package around. Why you had to go and fuck shit up?"

"You wasn't saying that shit when I bought you them purses and diamonds you sporting. With the money them mothafuckas pay us for them DVDs we ain't never got to sling again!"

"But you murdered that bitch and they still looking for her."

Silence.

Suddenly, Ice wrapped his hands around Dip's throat.

"Don't you ever say that mothafucking shit out loud again!" He said through clenched teeth. "I had to kill her because she could ID me." He squeezed harder. "You know that shit. You got a nerve considering how you did Kris."

When he removed his hand off her throat she said, "How *we* did Kris." she corrected him. "It wasn't just me who got rid of that nigga's body." She rubbed her throat. "You sure you ain't into this DVD shit just to fuck young girls?" She had hate in her eyes.

COLD AS ICE

"What you say to me?" he asked slowly.

"I mean...you always liked 'em young, Ice. How old is that girl you fucking now?" She paused, flopping down. "Seventeen?" She laughed. "You twenty-two years old, Ice...start fucking with girls your own age."

"She 20 and who I'm fucking ain't none of your business. Matter fact..." He continued as he snatched her purse and emptied its contents on the floor. "Since you got a problem with me and my biz, give me everything I bought yo ass."

"Get off of my purse!"

He shoved her backwards.

She tried to fight him but her 130-pound body was no match for his 190 pound one. When everything was on the floor he walked up to her and stripped her of all her jewelry, *diamonds* and rings. Then he tore off her red Edun blouse exposing her breasts. She covered herself with her arms and he grabbed her by the hair, opened the door and tossed her out.

"Ice, you—" He slammed the door in her face.

"Get outta my face!"

"Fuck you!" She yelled banging on the door. "I don't need your mothafucking ass! I don't need you for shit!" she continued crying uncontrollably.

Everyone in the neighborhood pointed as they witnessed Ice's mother outside of the door, naked.

"If I was your real mother..." she continued yelling. "You wouldn't be treating me like this. I should've left your ass on the street! I should've never took you in my house you reject!"

Ice heard what she was saying and up until now, he never treated her any differently. He remembered when Dip fed him all those nights his mother left him in the dressing room while she stripped at Louis

COLD AS ICE

Rouge, a strip club in DC. Jasmine always forgot to feed him and sometimes could care less if he was clean or safe.

Dip looked after him and even picked him up from Jasmine's from time to time so that he could get a shower and a hot meal. She couldn't have kids so she always had her sights on taking somebody else's and one day, for five hundred dollars, she got her wish. Sherrod was only five years old and for some money he belonged to her.

From that point on Dip looked after him, doing everything she could to make him cold as ice. Dip would do things like slap him if he cried and tell him only suckers showed emotions. She even introduced him to Canyon, one of her regulars at the club and he in turn introduced him to the glamour of the drug dealer's lifestyle. When he had the business down pat, Dip nicknamed him Ice, disposing of the birth name Jasmine had given him.

But Ice had a taste for something different. He got off on raping high school girls and making them cry. He'd lure them in his web from Myspace and release them when he was done raping them. Afterwards he'd hide his video recorder and place clips of his actions under the screen name, *Biggerthanitlooks* on the Internet, never showing his face.

Out of nowhere he started getting requests for the entire DVD set. Originally he sold them for two hundred dollars a pop in the black market. Before he knew it, Marcella, a Spanish broad from L.A., introduced herself by sending him her personal information. Ice was hesitant at first but she offered to wire him money to an offshore account he set up if more videos came her way.

From that point on, it was organized. He now had a *reason* to do what he always loved, rape. And with his mother holding the camera, it seemed he could get away with it all, until *one girl* snatched off his mask and saw his face. That same girl didn't make it home for dinner.

Knock. Knock. Knock. Dip knocked softer than before, waking Ice out of his thoughts of the past.

"What?" Ice yelled on the other end of the door.

"I'm sorry, baby," she said letting her guards down.

"I can't hear you?" He repeated as if he didn't hear her.

"I said I'm sorry, for everything." She wept. "Please don't do this to me. I raised you and I was wrong for talking to you the way I did. Let me in...*please*."

He smiled finally having won.

For the first time ever he broke down the one woman who taught him everything he knew, but he wasn't satisfied. Ice opened the door slowly and pointed to the floor. Not knowing what he meant, she walked in until he stopped her in his tracks, "Crawl, Dip."

"What?" She cried shirtless. "You...you can't be serious." She looked around to see who was watching.

Everyone was.

"If you want in this house I said get on the fucking floor and crawl."

Slowly she dropped to her knees and came inside. He slammed the door close, sat in the seat and watched her move toward him.

A smile rested on his face.

MAKING MATTERS WORSE

Pepper and Zykia were uncomfortable on the couch.

The phone rang just when JD was about to tell Pepper what he wanted from her. Instead of talking to her, he answered it. "Hello." His eyes widened. "Aw shit!" JD laughed. "Stop lying, nigga!"

"What...what man?" Izzy asked grabbing his arm. He was ear hustling and being nosey as shit. "What's going on?"

JD placed his hand on the phone. "Shut up, mothafucka!" He focused back on the call.

Zykia and Pepper sat on the couch wondering what was next.

"I wish I could've seen them fat ass titties!" JD continued on the call. "But look, I'ma get up with you later. I got business to handle over here. One."

When he hung up, he told his boys how Ice threw Dip out on the street, shirtless. JD and Izzy laughed hard as fuck but Khoury didn't.

When he was done he moved to Pepper. "Where's the DVD?" He got straight to the point.

"The DVD," she laughed. "I don't know what you talking about. What DVD?"

"Man stop fucking playing with me before I go down there and tell Ice what's really good!" JD yelled. "Now where's the fucking DVD? I want it."

Pepper looked at Zykia. "You told him about the DVD?"

Zykia nodded yes. "I didn't mean to. He heard me on the phone when I was talking to Ice."

Pepper glanced over at Jordan and his friends. Khoury was looking away while Izzy and Jordan stared her dead in the eyes. They had larceny in their hearts and she wanted to go home.

"I'm not gonna ask you again, Pepper," JD said. He leaned back and forth in a beat up leather recliner while waiting on her response. Slowly she reached into her book bag and pulled out the DVD. Jordan smiled, jumped up and snatched it from her hands.

"Go get my Playstation, Zy." He eyed the DVD like it was a winning lottery ticket for one hundred million.

Zykia grabbed the game system, hooked it up and placed the DVD inside.

The moment it came on Izzy and JD were into it like it was a gangster movie.

"Oh shit!" JD yelled as he saw the same gruesome scene the girls did a few days ago, of Ice's rape. Instead of being disgusted, he and Izzy were cheering Ice on while Khoury looked away. "That nigga's a beast!" JD continued.

"Yeah, man, he killing that pussy!" Izzy added.

After watching the complete DVD, JD turned it off and rubbed his hands together. "Whoa! This shit is major! When I heard baby girl over there on the phone I didn't think what ya'll had was this good. At first I ain't even know it was my little sister on the phone sounding all sexy and shit when she was blackmailing Ice," he joked. "But now I understand."

Zykia held her head down while Pepper grew so angry she felt like spitting in his face.

"It's like this," he continued. "After seeing that shit, I come to a realization."

"Did this nigga just say *realization*?" Izzy laughed looking for Khoury to co-sign.

He didn't.

"You know what I mean," JD replied. "Like I told my sister ya'll ain't asking for enough money. So I'm upping the anty. We want fifty G's instead of twenty-five and we splitting it forty for us and the rest for ya'll."

"Fuck you, JD!" Pepper yelled standing up. She was through with his fucking ass. She needed that money so she and her mother could leave the projects and here he was taking it all.

"Hold up, who you talking to?" he asked stepping toward her. He grabbed Pepper's arm and pulled her closer. Whispering in her ear he said, "You don't want to fuck with me, Reds. 'Cause next time I won't be trying to slide this dick in from the front," he continued rubbing his fingers between her legs. "I'll be taking that shit from the back." He released her.

"What you doing, man?" Khoury asked mad at how he was feeling Pepper up. "This going too far now."

Pepper looked at Khoury and then back at JD. "Chill out, man," he laughed. "I'm just having a little fun with her," he paused. "She know I'm teasing her right?"

Silence.

JD shrugged and focused on Zykia. "Fuck all that...call him back, sis. Tell that nigga the plan is still on for tonight but pack twenty-five more."

Zykia didn't move. "I'm not doing—"

"Move, bitch!" He screamed, "time is of the essence." He laughed looking back at Pepper licking his lips.

Zykia moved slowly toward the phone while Pepper stared him down trying to determine if she could take him or not.

"Whenever you feeling yourself," Jordan warned sensing Pepper's anger. "Make a move."

Just as Pepper was ready to smack him and deal with the consequences later, someone knocked at the door.

Everyone scattered.

"Oh shit!" Izzy yelled. "That nigga know!" He continued hiding behind the recliner. "He know and he gonna kill all of us."

"Yo, shut your bitch ass up, *Tenderheart*!" JD responded embarrassed by how Izzy was acting. "Now everybody calm the fuck down!"

When everyone was quiet and JD felt he was back in control, he bopped over to the door and saw two plain clothed officers through the peephole.

"It's the cops," he whispered. "Let me quarterback this shit. Chill out and sit back down." He advised. When they were in order he opened the door. "Can I help ya'll?"

"Yes," a female officer who resembled Vivica Fox said. "I'm officer Roberts and this is Officer Deville. Are your parents home?"

"Naw," he responded as he stepped outside closing the door behind him. "But what's up though?"

"You seen this girl?" The white officer who looked like Rosie O'Donnell questioned.

JD took the picture out of her hands. Without even looking he asked. "Why? She dead or something?"

Both officers frowned.

"That's a hell of a question to be asking." Officer Roberts replied looking at her partner.

"I don't know why," JD responded. "Ya'll don't come 'round here unless somebody's dead so you might as well keep it one hundred."

"She's missing…," Officer Deville said. "Now have you seen her or not?"

JD looked at the picture and his mouth dropped open at the girl he saw. It was the same one on the video.

His expression did not go unnoticed by the officers. "Well?" Roberts replied. "Seen her or not?"

"Uh...uh...naw. I ain't see her."

Officer Deville frowned. "Doesn't seem that way."

He shrugged. "You asked a question and I answered."

"Well if you do see her," she continued. "Call us." She handed him a business card. "Keep the picture and let your friends know."

"Is there a reward?"

The officers looked at each other and frowned. "Not at this time," Officer Deville frowned.

"Aight," he nodded still looking at the photo.

When they got in their car and drove off he entered the house, slowly. Everyone was waiting on him to give the word.

"Well?" Izzy said. "What they want?"

"They looking for that girl."

"What girl?" Khoury questioned.

"The one on the DVD."

"Oh shit!" they both responded. "What we gonna do?"

"Nothing but by the looks of things she's probably dead."

CHAPTER NINE

CAN'T TURN BACK NOW

It was two hours from the time they were supposed to pick up the money from Ice at the train station. Instead she was in the bed nervous and afraid. With JD involved she saw one ending to this story, death. For some reason she thought about what her mother said last week, before her plan to blackmail Ice.

Don't ever let people or situations change who you are. Everything will happen in time. God's time.

If only she'd listened she wouldn't be in this predicament now. She decided to call to hear her

COLD AS ICE

voice. Picking the phone up by the bed Pepper walked toward the living room. "What you doing, ma?"

"The same thing I was doing five minutes ago when you called silly," Grace laughed. "Working. Why you ask?"

Silence.

"*Pepper*...are you okay?"

"Yeah...uh...I'm fine." She flopped on the sofa. "I just wanted to hear your voice that's all."

"That's good but it doesn't sound like you're okay," she responded worried at her tone. "Are you feeling alright, Pepper? Go in the bathroom and get the thermometer to take your temperature."

"I'm fine, ma! Please don't worry! I was just calling to say I love you. You were always there for me and I wish I could've been more like you...honest."

"Pepper, you're scaring me."

"I'm serious, ma," she said sniffling. "I wish I waited for stuff to come my way instead of...instead off—"

"Pepper...I didn't tell you this earlier because I hoped it would go away." Her voice sounded anxious, like she'd been running. "But I want you to stay away from Ice, he's a problem."

"What?" Pepper said trying to be sure she heard what she did. "Why...why do you say that, ma?"

"Just stay away, Pepper. It isn't a request it's a demand."

Pepper took a deep breath. "Okay...I have to go, bye ma."

THE BIG PAYOUT

Ice stood in the middle of his living room preparing to hand over the money. His mother was with him. "You stuffed fifty g's in that bag?" Dip asked trying to be careful with how she talked to Ice. She didn't want to risk another altercation or being thrown out on the street.

"Yeah." He replied rolling up the edge of the McDonald's bag. "You got everything you need don't you?"

"Sure do." She stood up. "I'm all set."

"I'm talking *Everything,* Dip?" He asked again to be sure.

"Yes, Ice." She paused. "But do you actually think they're gonna give us the DVD?" She continued picking up her plastic bag. "I have a bad feeling about all of this."

"I don't know," he said hunching his shoulders. "Cuz either way somebody knows...and that means somebody has to die. Crystal's on that DVD, Dip. I have no choice."

"I know...that's why I'm worried." He paused. "Let's go." When they walked to the car, Ice saw Deadman laying down drunk as always, in front of his house.

"Yo, Dead," Ice yelled kicking him. "Yo, Dead!" He continued kicking him harder with his Timbs. "Get the fuck from in front of my house."

Dead barely lifted his head when he pushed him in his guts with his boots. "I...I'm moving," he said slowly clearly intoxicated.

Ice shook his head.

He and Dip were in the car with the key in the ignition when he came up with a plan. "Stay here. I'ma holler at Dead for a minute."

"Okay...but we don't wanna be late."

He looked at her and glared.

"I'm sorry," she swallowed. "I'll wait."

His plan was far fetched but was worth a chance. Since Dip was rolling with him to watch his back, nobody he trusted would be at the house to see the drop of the DVD off.

Nobody but Dead would.

Ice called Deadman just as he was trying to pull himself from in front of his house, slogging down the street. He was disgusted by how he moved. *Damn! This nigga been drinking too long.* Ice thought.

"Yo, Dead!" Ice yelled. "Hold up for a second."

Deadman turned around. "Wh...what?" His body swayed.

"What you sipping on tonight?"

"Sh...shit," he stuttered. "Whatever you buying?"

Ice reached in his pockets and pulled out fifty bucks. "The next round's on me."

"What's the catch?" Dead snatched the money before he had a chance to change his mind.

"No catch," he replied wiping his goatee. "And there's more where that comes from." He pointed at him. "On one condition."

"What's that?" Dead responded.

"I need you to keep a look out on my crib. If you see anybody pull up, write the tag number down."

Deadman nodded. "Okay," he laughed. "I'll put it in my planner." He continued laughing harder. He was so dirty Ice couldn't see his face. "I don't know if you took a look, lil man...but I ain't got no pen or paper."

Ice frowned. "You know what the fuck I mean, nigga! Remember as much shit as you can."

Dead nodded a little and Ice slapped him upside his head. "You getting this, fool?" Ice was starting to wonder if this drunk would even remember what he said five seconds from now let alone a few hours.

"Uh...yeah...sure...I got it," Dead swayed from side to side just to keep his balance. "But what you do?"

Realizing he was wasting his time because he was nothing more than a worthless alcoholic Ice said, "Fucked and murdered a young bitch. You gonna remember that?" He laughed before walking

away. "Drunk ass nigga!"

CHAPTER TEN

SECONDS FROM GREATNESS

"There he go," Izzzy said to Khoury as they sat outside of Addison Road Metro station, in the stolen blue Honda Accord that JD hotwired earlier. Both of them watched Ice pull up in his Aston and park in the lot. "Text JD and tell 'em that nigga here!"

Khoury was checking their surroundings and noticed Ice was by himself. He thought for sure that he'd have at least one person with him.

"Something's up," Khoury stated to Izzy. He'd sent the text to JD and was waiting on a response as he looked around.

"Why you say that?" Izzy asked. "So far so good."

"Cuz it don't feel right," he scanned his surroundings again. "Why Ice giving in so easy? I'd think he'd put up more of a fight when we asked for extra money."

"Cuz he's a fucking molester!" Izzy shrugged. "Either way I don't give a fuck. All I want is the dough."

Khoury wasn't buying it. There was something about his surroundings that messed with him. The normal watcher would see a girl strolling a baby, an old man and woman walking toward the escalators and a chick talking to some dude at the phone booth.

But he saw a set up.

COLD AS ICE

A few seconds later Khoury received JD's message which read, '*Affirmative*.' "He got it," Khoury advised placing his phone back in his pocket. "I sure hope he gets away with this."

"He will. It's a piece of cake," Izzy laughed. "And we about to be rich!"

GIVING UP IS SO HARD TO DO

Ice walked slowly up to the subway map posted on the wall. He tried to look around without showing his anger. But because he was a lover of time, he realized that with patience he'd get his revenge.

With the bag in his hands, he took a few sips from a McDonald's cup he was carrying and threw it in the trashcan. Afterwards he took one last look at the pedestrians before stepping on the escalators, fifty thousand lighter. As agreed, he strolled to his car and drove out of the station, without confrontation.

"That nigga's gone!" Izzy said sliding all the way down in the car seat when he saw Ice leaving. "He really rolled out! Oh shit!" Without wasting time, he called JD. "He's out, man!" He cheered. "Grab the dough, JD!"

"I already got it, nigga." JD advised.

When he got off his cell he looked at Khoury and said, "We 'bout to be paid!"

"That's how it looks," Khoury said unenthused.

COLD AS ICE

Izzy frowned. "You don't sound too happy."

"I'll believe it when I see it."

THE ROOT TO ALL EVIL

With the bag in tow, Jordan ran down the escalators. He had more money in hands than he'd ever seen in his young life. When he approached the exit doors he took two steps out, looked around and darted to the car.

Slamming the door shut he said, "Behold nigga's." He opened the bag to let them see the crumbled money. "We 'bout to get pussy for days on account of this shit right here! And we splitting it three ways."

Khoury frowned. "What about your sister and Pepper?" JD counted a few of the bills and Izzy helped.

"What about 'em?" JD shrugged.

"So you doing them like that?" Khoury continued.

"Did you honestly think I would give them bitches anything?" He chuckled. "Fuck them chicks!"

CHAPTER ELEVEN

CAN'T RUN BACK NOW

"Okay...I'm leaving now," Zykia said to Pepper who was sitting on the sofa. "They got the money and he wants us to make the drop."

"Why should we make the drop?" Pepper asked. "I don't trust it."

"Because I don't want Ice coming to look for us."

"Aight," Pepper responded. "But I want to tell you something."

"I don't know if I want to hear this," Zykia said as she grabbed her keys. "The last time you told me something you showed me that fucking DVD and it ruined my life." She sighed. "So unless it's important, I want you to save it until this is over."

They walked out the house.

"I made a copy," Pepper blurted out.

"For what?" She asked as she locked the door, her eyes widening. "WHY, PEPPER? I want this to be over!"

"I want it to be over too." Pepper replied. "But I thought about it, if we don't tell the cops, he'll get away with this. You heard what JD said. They're looking for this girl. What if she dead?"

"Don't say that, Pepper!"

"It's true!"

"Whatever you do," Zykia responded as they reached Old Lady Howard's fence. "I told you it was a bad idea to make a copy and to blackmail Ice so just leave me out of it." When they reached Pepper's

COLD AS ICE

house Zykia said, "Now you stay right here by the bushes. I'm gonna drop it off."

"Aight," she whispered looking around. "Be careful."

Zykia looked around and saw a few people doing regular shit. When the coast was clear, she crept past Deadman who as always, was passed out next to Ice's house. For some reason she had a feeling he was watching her. But when she turned around, his eyes were closed.

When she reached the steps to Ice's house, she placed the DVD in an old flower plant pot that hadn't been used for years and ran down the stairs and up to Old Lady Howard's house.

"Let's stay right here," Zykia whispered. "I'm not ready to go in the house just yet."

NEVER SAW IT COMING

At the train station, Dip stood by the phone booth and made her call. "You heard right, Ice," she said looking at JD and his friends whose faces she could not see because they were down too low.

"I can't believe this lil nigga was bold enough to fuck with me," Ice said with anger.

"Yeah well believe it," Dip responded. She was the lady talking to the man at the phone booth earlier and saw JD grabbing the money and going to the car where Izzy was waiting.

Before spotting them, when Ice let her out at the bottom of the block by the train station, she walked up to the phone booth by foot. This way Ice could appear to be by himself. And because she was wearing a black wig instead of her normal blond hair the boys didn't spot her. Their young ages and greedy nature also helped blind them.

"I'ma fuck them lil niggas up!" Ice spat. "Who was with 'em again?"

"Like I said I'm not sure but it looked like JD, Izzy and a third kid I couldn't recognize." She hailed a cab and got inside.

"Well did one of the niggas with him have dreads?"

"Couldn't tell." She told the driver where she was going and returned to the phone call. "I'm telling you he was low in his seat. I saw JD and Izzy for sure."

"Well where you at now?" Ice questioned.

"Just jumped in a cab."

"Cool," Ice responded relieved she was on her way back so that she could grab the DVD and he could go after his money. "Go straight to my crib and see if they left the DVD."

"Where you going?"

"Dro and Pipes on their way to meet me at that lil nigga's house."

"You got them involved?" Dip asked concerned.

"Yeah…but they don't know why they helping me murk these lil niggas," Ice advised. "That secret is still between me and you."

"Aight."

"Call me when you get the DVD. "

"Got it."

"I hope so," he said hanging up.

MONEY SPENT

Jordan, Izzy and Khoury made it back to JD's house safely and unharmed. "This shit was too easy," Jordan bragged. "I told ya'll we could come up on my sister and that chick."

"Yeah!" Izzy added, jumping on his dick as usual. "Let's divvy this shit up real quick 'cuz I already know what I'm buying."

"Maybe we shouldn't spend that dough just yet," Khoury advised. "Let's just give it a little time and lay low."

JD frowned. "Why not?" He asked. "We earned it."

"'Cuz if we just up and start dropping money out of nowhere, people are gonna start suspecting stuff." Khoury added. "But if we wait and let some time slide by we'll be good."

Izzy and JD looked at each other and broke out into laughter.

"This nigga's dumb," Izzy said.

"I'm serious, Izzy," Khoury continued. "JD, no offense but your moms is on drugs so you showing up with loot all of a sudden is kinda hot."

"Oh shit," Izzy laughed covering his mouth with his fist. "I think this nigga's going on your peeps!"

JD frowned. "Hold up…is you going on my moms?" He stood up and approached him.

"I'm being real with you," Khoury responded not backing down. "Ice ain't dumb, he's gonna be looking at everything and everybody now that he's out of fifty stacks. All I'm saying is let's be cool."

"Fuck you, nigga!" JD yelled pointing in his face. "Since you got a problem with this, you ain't getting none of it. How 'bout that." He continued spreading the money on the table.

"You know what…I don't want any of it. I'm out!" Khoury walked out the door but looked at them before leaving. "Just remember I warned ya'll."

"Nigga, get the fuck out my crib and lock my door before you shut it!"

Khoury slammed the door shut and Izzy rubbed his hands together and stuck his tongue out his mouth as he salivated over the money.

"I guess we splitting the pie two ways now," Izzy smiled.

"Yep…that's one unlucky mothafucka."

ALMOST OUT OF TIME

Pepper and Zykia were still by Old Lady Howard's house when they spotted Khoury moving in their direction. "Ain't that Khoury?" Pepper asked unsure because it was dark. "It looks like his dreads."

Zykia squinted a little. "Yeah...that's him," she confirmed.

"Where's his boys?" Pepper whispered. "I figured they'd be counting my money now."

"Khoury's cool," Zykia said under her breath. "If you noticed he ain't say shit when my brother was being greedy earlier. He don't seem like that kind of nigga."

Pepper thought about it for a moment. "Yeah...he ain't say shit period," Pepper said sarcastically. "Good or bad. Anyway he's still cool with JD so for real, I don't like him."

"I don't think ya'll want to go to your house now," Khoury advised approaching them. "JD's on a power trip."

"Well why you ain't with 'em?" Pepper interjected. "Since they your friends."

"'Cuz I'm not trying to be involved in all that,"
he said waving them off. "But I'll get up with ya'll
later." He was walking away until he stopped dead
in his tracks. Turning back toward them he said,
"Walk deeper under the bushes real slowly and
don't look across the street."

"Why?" Zykia asked frustrated with everything.
All she wanted was to go home and go to sleep.

"Yeah what's up?" Pepper added.

"Ice is on the other side of the street walking in
the direction of your house."

Asking no more questions the three of them
dipped all the way into Old Lady Howard's fence.
Thick trees, long grass and the unattended grounds
hid them well.

"Oh my God!" Pepper whispered looking
through the wired fence. "He must be looking for
us!"

COLD AS ICE

"Or us," Khoury replied.

"We dead," Zykia cried, pressing her hand down over her lips. "We all dead."

THE WRONG NIGGAS STASH

"Dem lil niggas in there," Dro responded as he peeped through JD's window watching them count Ice's money. He turned toward Ice. "How many you said we looking for again?"

"Two and a possible," Ice said, as he looked behind him making sure no one was coming. "You see my money?" Ice asked, two .45's in hand.

"Yep," Pipes replied. "Them niggas geeking like shit too."

Ice nodded. "Good, let's move in."

Without discussing the details, Dro kicked the door and Ice and Pipes followed.

SOMETHING TO CRY ABOUT

"Oh shit!" Khoury responded upon seeing Ice and his goons run up into JD's house. "Them niggas about to die!"

"Oh God!" Zykia responded moving toward the opening of the gate. "I have to go help him!"

Khoury grabbed her while she was kicking and screaming and Pepper helped him. "I'm gonna let you go but you have to listen, Zy," Khoury whispered. When he saw she was partially calm he took a deep breath. "If you go in there...he'll kill you too. I know it's fucked up but it's how it's gonna be."

"What about my brother?" She sobbed. "They gonna hurt him."

"He's dead, Zy and it's best you know that now," he said softly. "But I also know you ain't no good to him if you give up your life too. Let's just chill and see what happens."

FALLEN ON DEAF EARS

"I'm sorry, Ice," Izzy cried shaking his head from left to right. "This was Jordan's idea and I ain't want nothing to do with taking your money. I told him to leave me out of it but he wouldn't listen."

Without saying anything else, Ice took the butt of the gun and cracked Izzy's teeth out. Three rolled out onto the floor, roots still attached. Izzy fell to his knees holding his bleeding mouth.

Now he was silent.

COLD AS ICE

"Don't say shit unless I tell you to." He warned him, afraid Izzy in his hysteria would mention the DVD. As far as Dro and Pipes knew, this was a drug deal gone bad, nothing more and nothing less. "Is this all my money?"

"Yeah," JD replied as he farted in his boxers. "It's all there."

"Man, why you give these lil niggas that much money?" Dro asked.

"Yeah man?" Pipes confirmed.

"Later for that shit," Ice responded. "Don't concern yourself with my business."

They looked at each other and shook their heads.

"Its all there I promise," JD continued. "We ain't got the DVD though," Jordan cried as his softhearted friend lie helplessly on the floor. "You can count it if you want."

"*DVD?*" Dro and Pipes repeated simultaneously.

Ice looked at them and said nothing.

"I think I will make sure it's all there," Ice responded looking back at his men. "Count that shit, Dro."

Dro moved to the table and counted the paper as Pipes and Ice kept the burners on them.

"I counted fifty large," Dro advised.

"Fifty g's? Ya'll trying to play me?" Ice frowned. "Where's the rest of my money?" He cocked his gun.

JD's eyes widened. "It's all there!" He replied. "We only took fifty and every penny is there."

"Man, what the fuck is going on?" Dro asked more confused than ever. "They owe you more money, Ice or not?"

Ice looked at Pipes, Dro, JD and Izzy. With a sinister glare he said, "What's going on is this…"

BOOM! BOOM! BOOM! BOOM!

COLD AS ICE

Four bodies dropped and Ice took in the bloody scene. Taking the money off the table, he stuffed it back in the McDonalds bag and exited, with no witnesses standing.

WHEN SHOTS RING

Zykia cried in Khoury's arms when the shots rang out.

"Jordan!" She sobbed. "My brother's dead! OH MY GAWD my brother's dead!"

"Sssssshhhhhh," Khoury advised. "You gonna be okay.

Pepper was trying to hold her composure. She had to deal with the fact that this was all her fault. Had she never come up with the plan to blackmail Ice people would be alive. All she wanted was to get away from the projects and because of it she allowed greed to consume her.

And now it was too late.

Her best friend may have lost her brother and they could possibly lose their lives.

"There he goes," Khoury replied seeing Ice run away from the scene. "This nigga killed everybody. We gotta stay quiet!"

COLD AS ICE

HEARING VOICES

There he goes. Is what Ice heard on the other side of the street when he left JD's house.

When he looked around, he couldn't see anybody but was certain he heard voices. Folks usually got ghost when gunshots rang because no one wanted to be a witness so he wasn't surprised that the streets were vacant but still...where did the voice come from?

Going with his instincts he moved toward old lady Howard's fence.

Ice was all prepared to unload into the mini forest if need be.

"Who over there?" He asked, gun in hand as he crept across the street. Once there he pushed overgrown trees aside and peered into the thick mess. "I said who's in there?"

Silence.

Not satisfied he was preparing to go into the fence when he heard...*woof, woof, woof!*

Before he could get into the yard a dog charged the gate, teeth baring his way. "Oh shit!" He jumped back upon seeing a dog. "Fucking mut! I should shoot your ass."

THANK YOUR LUCKY STARS

When the dog came running out toward Ice it frightened the group cowering in the yard. They forgot she had a dog when they hid on her property. Old lady Howard let him out at night to keep thugs off her lawn, but as filthy as it looked, she didn't have anything to worry about.

The dog continued to bark along the length of the fence until Ice was out of sight. When he was gone Zykia made a movement and the dog heard them. Luckily they hopped the gate just before he bit them.

As the night progressed things began to get even more out of control.

CHAPTER TWELVE

EXCUSES IN THE FACE OF EVIL

"The cab broke down." Dip responded to Ice on the phone as he walked toward his house after killing four people.

"So basically you saying you ain't been here yet?" He continued approaching his steps.

"It wasn't my fault." Dip responded. "I'm tripping out as much as you are. One minute I'm on the way and the next..."

Ice hung up not needing to hear excuses. All he wanted was the DVD in his hands and a chance at normalcy. As he knew it anyway. He searched everywhere the yard including a flower pot he kept in front of his house that was used to stash drugs sometimes. With all of the searching, he still came up short.

"Where the fuck is it?" He said out loud.

He was preparing to walk back to JD's house thinking the DVD was there when he heard, "Looking for this?"

He turned around and saw Deadman holding the white DVD case in his hand, standing up straight as an arrow. His speech not slurred one bit.

"Aw shit," Ice laughed. "Let me find out your bum ass looked out after all." He moved toward him.

"Sure did," he responded. "Now it's time for you to pay me."

"Not a problem, old head," he replied snatching the case. "I got you."

COLD AS ICE

"When?" Deadman frowned.

"When hell freezes over," he laughed feeling relief wash over him. "But good looking out on this." He shook it. "It's time to celebrate."

He ran up his steps, turning his back on Deadman. He didn't hear the footsteps that were on his trail but he did feel a stinging sensation in his back. "What the fuck." It took him a minute but after some time Ice realized he had been stabbed in his back.

When he turned around he saw Deadman standing directly in front of him now and then he felt pressure in his stomach.

Ice was being sliced wide open.

He fell up against his door, eyes wide with fear.

"How does it feel?" Deadman asked watching him slide down the door, blood smearing against the frame.

Ice tried to pull his gun from his waist but didn't have the strength.

"What....did I...I do to you?" Ice asked touching his stomach wound, before looking at the blood on his hands. "I was gonna pay...pay you, man."

"Do you remember Crystal?"

"N...no," Ice lied, barely able to breathe.

Deadman stepped up to him and stabbed him again. Stooping down he took a deep breath. "Lie to me again, next time I'm slicing your throat. There's still time to call an ambulance to get you some help if you come clean now."

Ice suddenly noticed that Deadman was coherent.

"Again...do you know Crystal Hyatt?"

"Yeah, man...shit!" He replied giving into the pain.

"Good...now did you kill her...my daughter?"

Ice looked into his eyes, slowly slipping out of consciousness.

"No," Ice lied.

"Even on your death bed you check in for hell," Deadman responded. "But I saw what you did to my daughter on this DVD already. So it's okay. The last thing I want you to see is my face. I spent two months sleeping on the streets and in front of your house just to find out the truth. I lost my wife, my other daughter and even my house. And you know what, it was all worth it."

Not saying another word, he slit Ice's throat and left him on his own doorstep.

CHAPTER THIRTEEN

THE CALM AFTER THE STORM

"Y a'll take the last of that stuff and put it in the U-haul." Grace said to Pepper and Zykia as she stood in the living room.

"Okay, ma," Pepper replied as she and Zykia grabbed one of the boxes.

Today was the happiest day of Pepper's life. They were finally leaving 58th and although they weren't moving to a new house in Virginia, they *were* moving somewhere safe. Grace was renting an apartment in Laurel, Maryland and she convinced

Zykia's drug addicted mother to let her move with them.

"You want me to carry anything?" Khoury asked.

"Yes, baby, if you can lift those boxes over by the stove that will be good." When she hit the corner he stole a kiss from Pepper.

Grace shook her head. "I saw that!"

The two of them giggled and got back to business. Most of their things were inside of the truck when she heard, "Pepper."

She turned around and saw Deadman all cleaned up and standing before her. He looked like Morgan Freeman now that she could see his face. All tall and regal. "Deadman? Is that you?" Pepper questioned not believing her eyes.

"Yes, Pepper."

"Wow…you look…different." She stared him down.

"Thanks…I wanted to give you something I think belongs to you." He reached into his pocket and handed her an envelope. "Go ahead…open it."

She took the envelope not knowing what it was or why he was giving it to her. When she looked inside her mouth dropped. Enclosed were sixty one hundred dollar bills.

"What's this for?"

"It's some of the money from the night Ice was killed."

Pepper looked at him in fright. Up until that point she figured somebody robbed him for the money. "You killed Ice? Why?"

"That girl…on the DVD…was my daughter. And I've been sleeping out here for two months trying to get some answers because I knew he was responsible but no one would believe me, not even DC police." He took a deep breath. "I finally did something about it the night things kicked off."

"But you were sleeping on the ground everyday. Letting people kick you and...spit on you. How...How...?"

"It was hard, Pepper, but I had to know the truth. I got a lead that Ice knew something. But when I saw what kind of person he was, I knew he'd never tell me. So I came out here night after night. Eventually I got fed up and had my nephews run up in his place looking for clues. But one of them dropped the one thing I didn't even know existed, the DVD. That son of a bitch recorded it!"

"But...I don't get it," she responded still shocked. "How did you know I was involved?"

"I saw you and Zykia drop the DVD off. I was outside that night ,Pepper. So I put one and one together about the blackmail."

"What is your real name?"

He chuckled. "Craig Hyatt."

She hugged him tightly. So tight he could barely move. "Oh...thank you, Mr. Hyatt. Thank you so much!" She finally released him.

"I would've given you more but the rest is going to a foundation in my daughter's name." He looked around. "I'm glad ya'll getting out of here." He breathed deeply. "It's about time."

"Me too." She looked down at the envelope. "Thanks for everything...But can I ask you something?"

"Sure."

"Do you have the DVD?"

"No...I destroyed it. My family's been through enough. I told them I can't say how, but I know for certain she's in a better place. I don't want them involved in the media and I'd appreciate if you kept our secret."

"I will," she smiled. "Sure...whatever you want."

"Tell Zykia I said goodbye and you two be safe."

"We will."

When she watched Mr. Hyatt, get into the same van from the night Ice was robbed, she still couldn't believe her eyes. He loved his daughter so much that he played himself off as a bum just to find out the truth about her disappearance. She was still thinking about him when Dip rolled up on her.

"So you finally leaving 58th huh?" She asked from inside Ice's car.

Pepper nodded, her heart beating rapidly.

"You know what they say though," Dip started smoking a Black and Mild with the window down. "You can take a thief out the hood but it doesn't mean they'll live. Watch your back."

Pepper kept her eyes on Dip, lifted her shirt in the back and pulled out the copy of the DVD she held.

"And you watch yours." She said waving her copy.

Dip smirked. "I will Reds...I will." She pulled off.

"What she want?" Khoury asked kissing Pepper's cheek and watching her disappear up the road.

"Nothing, baby," she smiled tucking the DVD in the front of her pants. "Nothing at all."

The Cartel Publications Order Form

www.thecartelpublications.com
Inmates **ONLY** receive novels for $10.00 per book.
(Mail Order **MUST** come from inmate directly to receive discount)

Shyt List 1	_____	$15.00
Shyt List 2	_____	$15.00
Shyt List 3	_____	$15.00
Shyt List 4	_____	$15.00
Shyt List 5	_____	$15.00
Pitbulls In A Skirt	_____	$15.00
Pitbulls In A Skirt 2	_____	$15.00
Pitbulls In A Skirt 3	_____	$15.00
Pitbulls In A Skirt 4	_____	$15.00
Pitbulls In A Skirt 5	_____	$15.00
Victoria's Secret	_____	$15.00
Poison 1	_____	$15.00
Poison 2	_____	$15.00
Hell Razor Honeys	_____	$15.00
Hell Razor Honeys 2	_____	$15.00
A Hustler's Son	_____	$15.00
A Hustler's Son 2	_____	$15.00
Black and Ugly	_____	$15.00
Black and Ugly As Ever	_____	$15.00
Year Of The Crackmom	_____	$15.00
Deadheads	_____	$15.00
The Face That Launched A	_____	$15.00
Thousand Bullets		
The Unusual Suspects	_____	$15.00
Miss Wayne & The Queens of DC	_____	$15.00
Paid In Blood (eBook Only)	_____	$15.00
Raunchy	_____	$15.00
Raunchy 2	_____	$15.00
Raunchy 3	_____	$15.00
Mad Maxxx	_____	$15.00
Quita's Dayscare Center	_____	$15.00
Quita's Dayscare Center 2	_____	$15.00
Pretty Kings	_____	$15.00
Pretty Kings 2	_____	$15.00
Pretty Kings 3	_____	$15.00
Pretty Kings 4	_____	$15.00
Silence Of The Nine	_____	$15.00
Silence Of The Nine 2	_____	$15.00
Prison Throne	_____	$15.00
Drunk & Hot Girls	_____	$15.00
Hersband Material	_____	$15.00
The End: How To Write A	_____	$15.00
Bestselling Novel In 30 Days (Non-Fiction Writing Guide)		
Upscale Kittens	_____	$15.00
Wake & Bake Boys	_____	$15.00
Young & Dumb	_____	$15.00
Young & Dumb 2:	_____	$15.00
Tranny 911	_____	$15.00
Tranny 911: Dixie's Rise	_____	$15.00

COLD AS ICE

First Comes Love, Then Comes Murder	_____	$15.00
Luxury Tax	_____	$15.00
The Lying King	_____	$15.00
Crazy Kind Of Love	_____	$15.00
And They Call Me God	_____	$15.00
The Ungrateful Bastards	_____	$15.00
Lipstick Dom	_____	$15.00
A School of Dolls	_____	$15.00
Hoetic Justice	_____	$15.00
KALI: Raunchy Relived	_____	$15.00
Skeezers	_____	$15.00
You Kissed Me, Now I Own You	_____	$15.00
Nefarious	_____	$15.00
Redbone 3: The Rise of The Fold	_____	$15.00
Clown Niggas	_____	$15.00
The One You Shouldn't Trust	_____	$15.00
Cold As Ice	_____	$15.00

(**Redbone 1 & 2** are **NOT** Cartel Publications novels and if <u>ordered</u> the cost is **FULL** price of $15.00 **each**. <u>No Exceptions</u>.)

Please add $5.00 **PER BOOK** for shipping and handling.

The Cartel Publications * P.O. BOX 486 OWINGS MILLS MD 21117

Name: _____

Address: _____

City/State: _____

Contact/Email: _____

Please allow 5-7 <u>BUSINESS</u> days <u>before</u> shipping.

The Cartel Publications is <u>NOT</u> responsible for <u>Prison Orders</u> rejected, <u>NO</u> RETURNS and NO REFUNDS.

<u>NO PERSONAL CHECKS ACCEPTED</u>

<u>STAMPS NO LONGER ACCEPTED</u>

BY T. STYLES